Library of Congress Cataloging-in-Publication Data

Dematons, Charlotte. 1957-
 [Waar is Assepoester? English]
 Looking for Cinderella / Charlotte Dematons ; translated and
adapted by Leigh Sauerwein. -- 1st American ed.
  p. cm.
 Summary: When Hilda goes for a walk, she encounters storybook
characters who repeatedly mistake her for Cinderella and try to get
her to marry the prince.
 ISBN 1-886910-13-8 (alk. paper)
 [1. Characters in literature Fiction.] I. Sauerwein, Leigh.
 ill. II. Title
PZ7.D3915Lo   1996
[E] -- dc20   96-11515

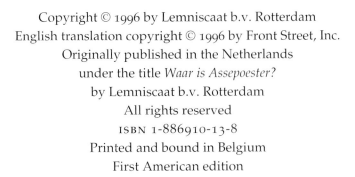

Looking for Cinderella

CHARLOTTE DEMATONS

Translated and adapted by Leigh Sauerwein

FRONT STREET 💲 LEMNISCAAT

ARDEN, NORTH CAROLINA

One Saturday in spring Hilda
noticed something strange about the
old windmill she could see from her
bedroom window.

The ancient vanes seemed to be slowly turning, first one way and then the other.
That's impossible, thought Hilda. The mill has been deserted for over a hundred
years! "I'm going for a walk, Mom!" she yelled.
"All right, dear, but be back before dinner!"

Hilda hurried along the narrow road that led to the old mill. Soon she noticed a small figure in red jumping up and down and waving.

As she got closer she could hear the girl shouting, "Hurry, oh, hurry up, please! Everyone is waiting!"

"Cinderella!" exclaimed the girl when Hilda walked up to her.
"Where in the world have you been? We were so worried!"
"My name is Hilda," said Hilda.
"Well, Cinderella, I have another name, too," answered the girl. "But *everyone* calls me Little Red Riding Hood!"

"I don't have another name.
Just Hilda," said Hilda.
But the little red girl didn't seem to
hear her. "How odd you look today,
Cinderella!" she exclaimed. "But never
mind, let's go!"
And taking Hilda firmly by the arm,
she led her into the mill.

"I found her! I found her!" shouted Little Red Riding Hood as she entered the mill with Hilda behind her. There was a huge crowd inside. Everyone was staring at Hilda, whispering and pointing. Then a prince, holding a gleaming delicate slipper, stepped forward, and a hush fell over the crowd. "The girl whose foot this shoe fits will be my bride!" he declared.

Before Hilda could say a word, Red Riding Hood had undone the shoelaces on
Hilda's left sneaker and slid the glass slipper onto her foot.

"It fits her perfectly!" Red Riding Hood cried.

Everyone in the mill sighed with relief.

"Good job, Riding Hood!" exclaimed a dwarf. "Now let's all get back to work."

And suddenly Hilda was alone with the Prince.

"My dearest Cinderella," he murmured, bowing and offering her his arm.

"I was so afraid I would never find you."

"But sir," stammered Hilda, looking down at the golden slipper on her foot.
It felt terribly loose and was really much too big for her. "Your majesty,"
Hilda began again. "This slipper is too . . . "
But the Prince didn't seem to hear her. "We must go now," he said softly.

He lifted Hilda onto a beautiful white horse and they rode deep into the forest.
As they rode, the trees seemed to be whispering something Hilda could not quite
understand. Suddenly two doves cried out:

"Coo roo! Roo coo!
There's room in the shoe!
Your bride, oh Prince,
still waits for you!"

The Prince looked down at Hilda's foot. He seemed to wake from a dream.
"You're not Cinderella!" he shouted at Hilda.
"Of course I'm not!" Hilda shouted right back at him. "I'm Hilda!"
The Prince helped her down off the horse.
"I must hurry now!" he cried, and he rode away shouting, "Oh where can she be?"
"You forgot your slipper!" called Hilda. But the Prince had disappeared.

Hilda put the shoe carefully into her
knapsack. I guess it's up to me to find
Cinderella, she thought to herself.
Suddenly a sharp stick poked her in
the stomach.

"Cinderella, you wretch!" croaked an
old witch who had appeared out of
nowhere. "Did you steal my cat?"

"I certainly did not!" said Hilda.
"And my name is Hilda!"

But the witch didn't seem to hear her.

"Come along at once and help me look
for him," she ordered.

Hilda followed her down a narrow,
winding path.

"Here Kitty! Here Kitty!" called the witch. "All this commotion has upset the poor thing."

Suddenly Hilda smelled gingerbread baking, and Hansel and Gretel came running up to her. "Have some gingerbread while it's still warm!" Hansel said.

"Snow White and the seven dwarfs are baking us a lovely new roof," explained Gretel. "That old gingerbread was so stale you could break your teeth on it."

"Here, Kitty! Here, Kitty!" croaked the wicked witch over by some bushes.

"I'll go look for your cat," offered Hilda, munching on the soft, warm gingerbread.

"What does the cat look like?"

"It's a black cat, of course!" laughed Hansel.

"Good-bye, Cinderella!" called Gretel. "Watch out for Riding Hood's wolf. I think he's lurking around here somewhere."

Hilda had just swallowed the last bite of gingerbread when she heard a sound like thunder. Was a storm coming? She hid behind a large boulder. There was the thunder again!

Hilda bumped into something and turned around. A little boy was putting one very small foot into an enormous boot. The boot began to shrink. It shrank and shrank until it was just the right size. An instant later the boy had the other boot on too. Hilda stared at him, thinking fast.

"You must be Tom Thumb!" Thunder rumbled over them.

"And that noise . . ." she gasped. "That must be the sleeping giant!"

"You got it, sister," said Tom Thumb calmly.

"He's right on the other side of this rock.

By the way, the old fellow is going to wake up now."

"I'm not your sister! I'm Hilda!"

But Tom Thumb didn't seem to hear her.

A mountainous shadow had fallen over them.

"Better start running now, kid!" yelled Tom Thumb.

Hilda screamed and took to her heels, but the giant was right behind her.
The pounding of his feet made the ground tremble. As he howled and roared,
she could feel his breath in her hair like a hot wind.
Faster, faster! she cried to herself.

She could hear Tom Thumb laughing from somewhere. He was yelling at the monster.
"You tub of guts!" he yelled. "You big-bellied blob of blubber!"
But of course he had the seven-league boots, she remembered. He didn't have anything
to worry about, the brat! And soon he was out of sight. Hilda ran and ran and ran . . .

Finally Hilda could no longer feel the ground shaking or hear the giant's terrible roaring. But she ran a little farther just the same, deeper into the forest. Suddenly she came upon a stone gateway. Everything was very still and quiet.

On the other side of the gate there stood a blue and gold coach drawn by two sleek horses. The coachman leaped down at once. "If you please, Miss Cinderella," he said, opening the carriage door.

"My name is Hilda," said Hilda wearily as she clambered in. But the coachman had already shut the carriage door and didn't hear her. He drove Hilda to a vast and beautiful house. But no one seemed to be home. Everything was very quiet as she walked through all the rooms. From time to time she heard a faint rustling, which she followed until she noticed a ladder leading to the attic. The trapdoor at the top of the ladder was open.

What a strange attic, thought Hilda, looking around.

There was no dust, there were no cobwebs. Everything had been scrubbed clean and the air smelled of soap.

"Hello! Is there anyone here?" she called softly.

Then, in a far corner of the attic, she saw a beautiful girl on her hands and knees scrubbing the floor.

"Cinderella!" cried Hilda.

"Yes? Who are you?" asked the beautiful
girl, tossing back her long blond curls.

"I'm Hilda. But everyone thinks I'm you!"

"Isn't that silly!" said the girl, laughing,
as she rose to her feet. And Hilda laughed
with her.

"I brought you your slipper," said Hilda.

"And I do wish you would go and find the
Prince so that I can go home!"

"Where do you live, dear?" Cinderella asked.

"Beyond the mill," answered Hilda,
"over the bridge, past the old elm,
and all the way into the town."

"Run down and jump into the coach," said Cinderella. It will take you home."

But just after passing the mill, the pretty carriage slowed down and came to a stop.

"I cannot take you any farther, miss," said the coachman politely.

And so Hilda hopped down, waved at the coachman,
and walked the rest of the way home.

"Hilda, I'm glad you're back!" called her mother. "We had a visitor this afternoon. Run and look on your windowsill!"

A big black cat looked at Hilda.

He seemed very pleased with himself. Hilda picked up the silky black creature.

"There you are," she whispered into his ear. "Do you know who that cat belongs to,
dear?" called her mother. "Don't worry, Mom," replied Hilda, smiling and listening
to the deep purring. "I'll take him home tomorrow."